Jingles
Lost Her Jingle

FAITH EDITION

ISBN: 9780991084104

King's Treasure Box Ministries, Cumming, GA

Illustrations by Bob Biedrzycki
Art Direction, Design, Illustrations Embellishments:
Steven Tyrrell / tyrrellcreative.com

A Princess Finds Truth and Joy After Sexual Abuse

Jingles
Lost Her Jingle

Tammy Kennedy
Illustrated by Bob Biedrzycki

Dedication

I dedicate this book to "my brotha from anotha motha," Michael Goldstone, who taught me there are so many men who are nothing like Mr. Finks. Michael, you showed me that men can be faithful because of your love for Deb. You showed me men can be loyal because of your love for your family. You showed me men can be honest because of your integrity within your home and church. You showed me men can be generous because you give so much away. You showed me men can be dedicated because of your hard work as a business owner. Most importantly, you showed me men can be safe because you love me with the biggest brother-heart a sister could ever have. Thank you for being you!

Acknowledgements

Writing this book has not been a solitary endeavor. Each chapter has been shaped and transformed by the constructive criticism of loved ones around me. Additionally, being whole enough to write such a book has not been a solitary endeavor either. My Heavenly Father began putting princess helpers in my life from birth.

Cathy Vaughn – You made this book possible! Your faith, friendship and love for the last 24 years have caused a healing in me that no therapist could duplicate. I love you so very much!

Mike and Deb Goldstone – You adopted me into your family and I'm never leaving! I have learned so much from you, and of course from Grammy. Thank you for allowing me to live in a beautiful castle while the King was preparing me for the next adventure. I love you so much!

To My Inner Circle Princesses - Dawn, I'll never have another BASS like you! Nanci, my beautiful Big Head. Jen, you inspire me to keep running the race and fighting the fight. Merylee, you've believed in my healing and in the Father's purpose for my life from the start. And Lu, you've taught me well. Thank you!

The most important people in my royal family to be acknowledged are the board members of The King's Treasure Box Ministries.

Nancy Roy – There would be no *Jingles Lost Her Jingle* book without you because there would be no princess to write it! You saved my life and I love you as much as any adopted daughter could love her adopted mom. Thank you for all your hard work in making this book possible and in helping form The King's Treasure Box Ministries.

Debbie McClain – There would be no *Jingles Lost Her Jingle* book without you because this princess is poor, has limited computer skills, has even less grammar skills, and has a huge need for a Princess BBB. Thank you for your friendship, the fun you create, and the resources and intelligence you share. I love you so much.

Muna Worku – There could be no *Jingles Lost Her Jingle* book without you because I would never have survived those hospital years without you. I'm sorry I put you through so much when we were roomies but God handpicked you to help me choose to live. I love you with the biggest sister heart a princess could have!

Fiseha Asfaw – And last but never least, I want to acknowledge my new brother who is covering us in prayer every day. We love you!

Contents

How to Use This Book

YOUR ROYAL ASSIGNMENT AS A PRINCESS HELPER

This book is oriented to girls ages 6 - 12 who have experienced sexual abuse. First read the book from cover to cover on your own to determine whether or not you can handle the material. You will also want to begin using the resource section for assistance before you begin helping your princess heal. Build your own support network fast. **This book is not meant to help you be the therapist.** Your child just needs you to be supportive and to listen.

Please read the Do's and Don'ts before starting the Jingles story.

PLEASE read the *Do's and Don'ts* in the appendix and encourage the rest of her support system to read it as well.

Read *Jingles Lost Her Jingle* to your little princess. Before you begin, tell her you found a storybook that might help her. Reassure her, let her know you love her, and want to help her with the pain. Let her know that parts of this special book will be fun and that you are going on an adventure together to help Jingles fight some monsters.

Get creative - *The Lie* chapters, where you will spend most of your time, are the most important. As someone who loves and knows her best, you will be highly effective in helping her challenge her beliefs about the abuse. Talk about the lies Jingles believes throughout the story. Use the Lie Monsters as a tool to help your princess relax, find fun in the discussion and to sort out truth from lies. You can make a "Sword Of Truth" with cardboard and foil; pretend you are fighting Lie Monsters together. Your princess' story will be different from Jingles', but there will be similarities. Certainly the feelings will be very similar. Princess Gracie will be there to help guide the dialogue. She represents the helpers God sends to assist us during our healing journey: a counselor, a priest/pastor, a good friend, etc. Together you will help Jingles fight the Lie Monsters who come to tell her that the abuse was her fault, that she is bad, and that she is now dirty. You will be great lie detectives.

NOTE: If you are a survivor of sexual abuse, and have not dealt with your own brokenness, *I strongly urge you to get help now*! You cannot walk her through this process as effectively without support and healing yourself. You may believe the same lies your sweet little princess believes. I care about you too!!

A NOTE OF ENCOURAGEMENT

This will be a hard journey for your family, but many treasures can come from pain. Get all the help you can afford and fight to get even more. You need the support and so does she. My purpose here is to empower parents or safe loved ones to know how to talk with their child about what happened without causing more damage. Even the most wonderful parents often do not know how to handle this topic.

A faulty belief system hinders us from walking in freedom, feeling loved, and knowing our standing in the King's eyes. Lies keep us stuck in the past and keep us sick. It's time to discover the truth and experience all the King has planned.

For most of my adult years, I carried a faulty belief system in my mind and heart until friends, family, my church, and counselors helped me sort out the lies I believed. The shame and guilt I stored inside affected my relationships, my career, and my goals. I get angry when I think about how many years it took me to recover, but I get excited knowing it is possible, and with early intervention the process can take much less time.

Believing lies hinders us from: walking in freedom, feeling loved, and knowing our standing in the King's eyes. Believing lies keeps us stuck in the past and keeps us sick. My hope and prayer is that your princess learns the truth, recovers as quickly as possible, finds her jingle very soon, and then discovers she can experience all that the King has planned for her life.

CHAPTER 1

Jingles Lost Her Jingle

Jingles was a very happy little girl. Just like her name, she had a jingle in her heart. She was happy in the morning when she saw the blue sky and the bright sun. She was happy when her mom let her pick out her favorite jingly clothes.

Jingles was a very happy girl and always had a jingle in her heart.

She was happy when her mom bought her favorite jingly cereal with just the right amount of marshmallow stars. And Jingles was especially happy when her dad came down to say good morning before she left for school. He works nights so she does not see him much except on weekends, but even then, he's too tired to play games or go places together.

Jingles was also very happy when she arrived at school each morning and got to see Stayshia. They have been best friends since 1st grade. Then Jingles was happy when the teacher cancelled the math test until the next day because Jingles was not sure she remembered her multiplication tables.

Jingles was also happy when they served pizza for lunch, but she was almost not too jingly inside when she saw the peas touching her pizza. Jingles did not like peas, but she got her jingle back when she saw that the peas just rolled off and didn't make the pizza taste different.

Jingles was most excited on the Fridays when her best friend Stayshia invited her for a sleepover. This next weekend, Stayshia says her stepdad has a special surprise for them. Mr. Finks always plans a fun event

and makes them laugh. Jingles wishes her dad spent time with her like Mr. Finks, but her dad works long hours and sleeps a lot. Jingles always has a great time with Stayshia and Mr. Finks. *Wow*, thought Jingles, *this will be the most jingly day ever!*

When Jingles arrived at Stayshia's house, she gave Mr. Finks a big hug and said, "Thank you for hav-

Mr. Finks said he had a special surprise for them.

ing me over." Then Mr. Finks served the girls warm chocolate chip cookies for a snack. Mr. Finks always gives Jingles special gifts or treats and he asked about their class assignments and told them he had a surprise movie for them later. After their snack, they had a fun pillow fight and everyone laughed until their sides hurt. Mr. Finks gave the girls a few more cookies and said, "You will really like this movie." Jingles could hardly hold in her jingly excitement. She loved

Mr. Finks and felt safe and cared for in his home. Mr.
Finks put the movie in the player and sat between
Stayshia and Jingles on the sofa. At first, Jingles was
excited because it looked like a movie about two girls
who were best friends just like she and Stayshia.

Suddenly, Jingles' happy jingle started to fall right out of her tummy. The girls on the TV screen began taking their clothes off. Jingles thought maybe they were going to take a bath, but that is not what they did.

Jingles' happy jingle started to fall right out of her tummy.

Jingles' happy jingle started to fall right out of her tummy.

Jingles' tummy was really starting to hurt, and she looked at her friend Stayshia. Stayshia was staring at the movie, but she looked like she did not see anything. She was staring straight ahead in a weird way. It was like she changed into a zombie or something.

Then Jingles looked at Mr. Finks, and his hand was between Stayshia's legs. Jingles was very confused, but Mr. Finks assured Jingles that Stayshia loved to play this game every afternoon and that she was going to like it too. Jingles could not understand why Stayshia had never told her about the "game" she

played with her stepfather. Mr. Finks began explaining that he has grown to love Jingles just as much as he loves Stayshia and he wants to show her how to love in a very special kind of way.

Jingles wanted to run and hide, but her feet would not move.

Mr. Finks told Jingles that she was pretty, but Jingles felt very ugly now. He told Jingles that she was very special and that he wanted to be her special friend. Jingles DID NOT FEEL SPECIAL! Jingles wanted to run and hide, but her feet would not move. Jingles had never felt fear in her tummy like this before.

Then everything got worse for Jingles! Not only were Stayshia and Mr. Finks touching each other's private parts, Mr. Finks began touching Jingles under her skirt. He said, "This is what good girls do,

and you are a very good girl." Jingles did not feel like a good girl. She felt very dirty inside and very embarrassed.

No one had touched her there since she was a baby when she needed her mom's help. Mr. Finks told Jingles she could not tell anyone about their special game today because it would make Stayshia get in big trouble, and she would be taken to a bad and dangerous place called a foster home. He said this was a "special secret" and no one could know about it, not even her mom or dad. Jingles loved Stayshia so much and would never want her to move away, and especially not to a dangerous place.

Mr. Finks made Jingles afraid to tell anyone or there would be trouble for her and Stayshia.

Mr. Finks also told Jingles that he knew she liked the way her body felt when he touched her. He said, "You don't have to feel bad about what we are doing because you are almost a big girl and it's okay between special friends. I knew you wanted me to touch you like this because of that big hug you gave me when you got here and the smile you gave me when you were eating the cookies. Then you flirted with me while we played with the pillows."

"I know you wanted me to touch you..."

Jingles tried to think about something else while she was sitting on the sofa, anything that might take her mind off the movie and Mr. Finks doing so much touching.

She knew she was getting older because her ninth birthday was coming up in just four months. Jingles tried to imagine having a fun birthday party.

But she could not find her jingle, even when she thought about the cake, her friends coming and the games.

Jingles totally lost all her jingle that day!

Jingles thought, *I never want to play another game or eat cake or have friends over or anything.* Jingles totally lost all her jingle that day!

CHAPTER 2

Believing Lies

How can we help Jingles get her jingle back? Will you help her? One of the problems is this—Jingles believes a lot of lies. Mr. Finks did not tell her the truth and Jingles thought adults always told the truth.

Let's go on an adventure to discover the truth and help Jingles get her jingle back!

I'd like to introduce you to Princess Gracie. The good King in Heaven sent her and He gave her special powers. One of her powerful gifts is being a super-duper Lie Detector. This skill is very important because there is a Master Deceiver[1] here on earth who has come to steal, kill and destroy the King's children.[2] The Master Deceiver sends lying monsters to keep us away from the King who wants to adopt us. Princess Gracie uses clues to find the Master Deceiver's lies and then sorts out the truth. Knowing the truth can make us all feel much better. Maybe you have heard someone say, "The truth will set you free." [3]

"You will know the truth, and the truth will set you free."

John 8:32

This means believing a lie keeps us stuck and prevents us from enjoying all the little things we usually enjoy every day. Believing a lie makes us feel very sad. The King and Princess Gracie want you, Jingles, and Stayshia to be able to run with the wind and play and learn and laugh and grow and be all that the King made you to be. He has had a plan to rescue you all along because He loves you so much.[4] The real truth

The King is good all the time and loves you.

is everyone who has told the King they want to be adopted by Him are considered royalty and He has made many promises to those who love Him. If you want to be one of the King's kids, just pray the special prayer on the scroll and tell Him how you feel. It really is that easy!

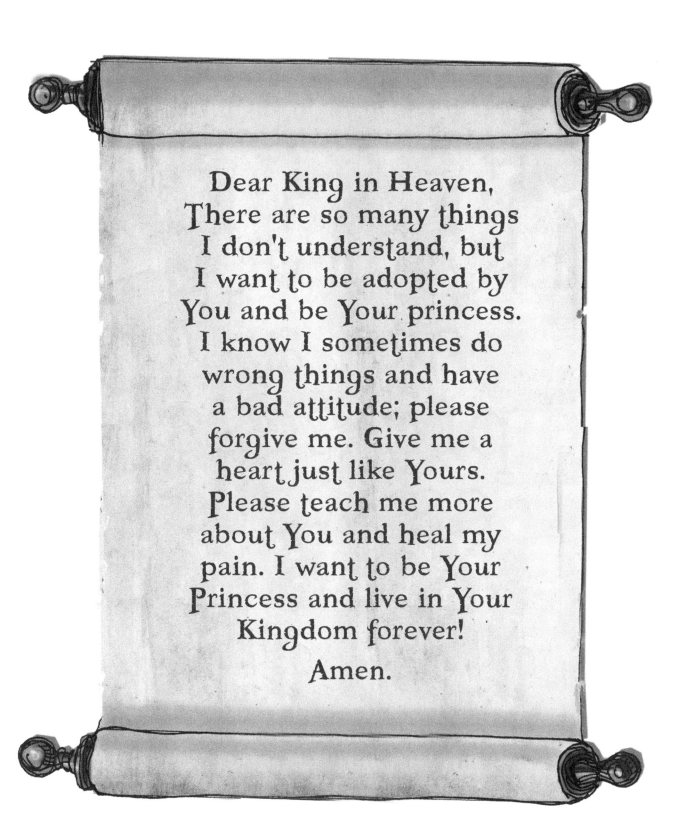

Dear King in Heaven,
There are so many things
I don't understand, but
I want to be adopted by
You and be Your princess.
I know I sometimes do
wrong things and have
a bad attitude; please
forgive me. Give me a
heart just like Yours.
Please teach me more
about You and heal my
pain. I want to be Your
Princess and live in Your
Kingdom forever!

Amen.

Now you are a princess as well!

Did you know the King is very angry with Mr. Finks for hurting Jingles? He said in Matt. 19:14 of His royal decree, "Don't hurt my children because I want them to come to me and I want to give them my kingdom."[5] Even if Mr. Finks never goes to jail, the King will make sure he has consequences for what he did to Jingles.

Not only will the King give back to those wounded by the Master Deceiver what was stolen, He will also send help and blessings so that they can heal and find joy again. One of the main ways the Master Deceiver steals our joy is by planting lies in our precious brains so that we feel lousy and yucky.

No worries though! The King sent Princess Gracie to help Jingles figure out the lies and discover the truth. Can you please help Princess Gracie and Jingles? I bet you're great at looking for clues and figuring things out.

Jingles feels very defeated because the Master Deceiver sent four Lie Monsters to attack her.

Shamer's Lie: "You are bad."

1) Shamer is the Lie Monster who whispers, "You are bad," in Jingles' mind and it causes her so much pain. Once she listens to the lie and does not defeat it, she then tells herself "I am bad." This Lie Monster wants Jingles to hate herself and hate the King who created her. Shamer tries to prevent Jingles from seeing the treasure she is to her family, her friends and her Father the King. He wants her to wear a mask like he wears so she never lets people know her real self; she will pretend to be someone she thinks is better. Shamer wants Jingles to believe she is now damaged because of what Mr. Finks did to her. This is a lie!

Guiltizar's Lie:
"It was your fault."

2) Guiltizar is the Lie Monster who repeats, "It was your fault," in Jingles' mind and heart every day. He wants to steal her joy forever by trying to convince her that what Mr. Finks did was her fault. If Jingles listens to his lies and does not defeat him, she will believe the lie and tell herself, "It was my fault." The guilt that comes after believing this lie is so painful; it steals our joy big time!! Jingles will then feel guilty about almost everything and believe she only deserves punishment. The King says Jingles is not guilty and she is His precious daughter.[6] Can you and Princess Gracie help her believe the truth?

Ickylamar's Lie: "You are dirty."

3) Ickylamar is the Lie Monster who whispers, "You are dirty," in Jingles' mind so often that poor little Jingles wants to live in a bathtub filled with super-powered soap bubbles and never come out. Ickylamar wants her to feel permanently yucky and dirty because of what was done to her. If she believes Ickylamar's lies, she will begin repeating the lie, "I am dirty," in her sweet mind. The Master Deceiver and Ickylamar are so cruel and they tell huge lies. They know the truth, that the King's royal decree says she is squeaky clean and very precious.[7] Her Father and King in Heaven adopted her and made her that way! Can you and Princess Gracie help Jingles fight this nasty Lie Monster?

Confusia's Lie:
"You liked it."

4) Confusia is the Lie Monster who causes our thoughts to be so muddlefuddled. She is a snake who is the master of mixing everything up in our minds. Her forked tongue is capable of telling nasty lies mixed with the truth so that any princess would be confused. She may whisper, "You liked it," in Jingles' mind to trick her into believing lies. Unfortunately, the Master Deceiver is smart. He made Confusia to look fun and sound kind so that the King's children will listen to her. Confusia's hypnotizing and friendly voice is a really mean attack from the Master Deceiver. If Jingles believes a whopper lie such as, "I must have liked it," she could be permanently sad. She will believe there is no hope in getting her jingle back or ever being loved again. Feeling hopeless, Jingles may make poor choices the rest of her life.

So heed this warning from the King: Watch out for this evil serpent cuz she's devious and mean.

You can help Princess Gracie and Jingles defeat the Lie Monsters with the Sword of Truth.

Let's look at the story and help Jingles find the truth. Princess Gracie and Jingles can defeat the Lie Monsters with the Sword of Truth. In 2 Cor. 10:4-6 of the King's decree, it says the weapons formed against us from the enemies are thoughts implanted in us that are not true.[8] In this battle, we must only listen to and believe what the King says.

CHAPTER 3

Lie #1
"I Am Bad"

Lie Monster number one, Shamer whispers, "I am bad," in Jingles' mind all day. This Lie Monster is very cruel and wicked. He tells such awful lies. When a precious princess feels she is bad, she won't go to her Father the King because she feels ashamed. She will hide her thoughts and feelings from her family, her friends and her Father the King.

Shamer makes you keep secrets and feel ashamed.

The lies that she believes will make her feel very sad and all alone. If Jingles hides from The Father who created her and all the people who love her most, they can't help her see that she believes lies; they can't help her learn the truth. The truth is that she is precious and the King made her carefully and wonderfully according to His decree in Ps. 139:14.[9] He adores her and nothing will ever change that.[15]

The truth is that Jingles is precious and the King made her carefully and wonderfully. He adores her and nothing will ever change that.

Before Princess Gracie helps Jingles discover the truth, let's look at how Shamer tells lies to princesses like Jingles. On page 6, Mr. Finks said, "You will really like this movie," so when Jingles remembers the movie she feels shame and embarrassment. She remembers watching the little girls on the screen with curiosity. Jingles thinks to herself, *Mr. Finks was right;*

Shamer wants Jingles to feel so much shame that she hides behind a mask like him.

I must have liked the movie since I sat there and watched the whole thing. The movie made Jingles feel ashamed in her heart, but she watched it anyway. That's when Jingles decided, "I am bad!"

Shamer is one of the cruelest and strongest Lie Monsters! He wears a mask and he wants Jingles, who also is a princess like you, to feel so much shame that she hides too. Let's crush his power by getting his lies out of our head. Get out your princess sword!

But how do you fight a Lie Monster? This monster is very big and looks very strong, and Jingles believes that there is no way that she can ever be "good" again. Princess Gracie fights the Lie Monsters by finding the truth, and there isn't a Lie Monster born that can survive the truth!

What do you think the truth could be? Do you think Jingles is a bad girl?

Princess Gracie says, "Just because Jingles obeyed an adult who asked her to watch the movie and told her she would like it, does not mean it was her fault that she watched the movie; it does not mean she liked the movie. Watching the movie did not make Jingles a bad girl. Precious and smart girls like you, Stayshia, and Jingles, are very curious about bodies and growing up and having friends and all sorts of things. Your curiosity means you are smart girls who are exploring the world around you. It is the adults' job to help you explore safe and good things."

"If someone touches you or makes you touch them, it is never your fault!"
-The King

Princess Gracie says, "Let's look for clues to find the truth." We have to stop Shamer the Lie Monster fast before he takes away all the music that Jingles holds in her heart. He will try to make Jingles believe the lie that she is bad; he will try to make her hide behind a mask like him and, if he wins, then she will hate the precious princess she was created to be. We don't want Jingles to suffer anymore from Shamer's lies so let's hurry and find the clues. Go back to pages 6 - 14.

CLUE Who put the movie into the DVD player?

CLUE Who sat between Jingles and Stayshia so he could touch both girls?

CLUE Page 10 says, "Jingles wanted to run and hide, but her feet would not move. Jingles had never felt fear in her tummy like this before." If Jingles wanted to run, does that mean she wanted to watch the movie?

CLUE Why do you think her tummy hurt so bad?

CLUE What do you think Jingles was feeling if she wanted to hide?

CLUE Who do you think behaved badly?

TRUTH Mr. Finks told Jingles that Stayshia liked the touching game every day after school. During the movie, the fact that Stayshia would not look at anyone, would not smile, would not talk, and that her face showed great sadness means she did not like what was happening. Mr. Finks told a huge lie when he said, "Stayshia likes this game." **The truth is Stayshia hates it when her stepfather touches her and makes her touch him.**

TRUTH Mr. Finks already had the movie to show Jingles and Stayshia before that day. He planned to show this movie to them and he was the adult responsible for keeping both girls safe, happy and secure. He served a yummy snack and started a fun pillow fight as a way to convince Jingles that the new touching game would be fun also.

TRUTH The fact that Jingles felt so uncomfortable, so scared, so nervous, and that her tummy hurt so bad shows that she did not like what was happening one bit!!

TRUTH Mr. Finks was the one who behaved badly and he was the one who made the bad choices. His behavior was very wrong; he knew it was very wrong, because he told Jingles to keep their new game a secret. The King is extremely angry with people who hurt His children.[10]

TRUTH Princess Gracie says, "I just spoke to my Father the King, and He said, 'You, Stayshia and Jingles were carefully and wonderfully made.[9] You are precious to me and you are precious to your family and friends. It has never been My plan that you would be hurt in any way,[11] but you live in a world where people do get hurt. You were exposed to something ugly, but that does not make you bad. You are good and I love you very much!' "

Princess Gracie says, "So let's stop Shamer the Lie Monster. Pick up your Sword of Truth and say out loud, 'I AM GOOD!' Say it louder. 'I AM GOOD.' The children in China can't hear you yet. Say, 'I AM GOOD' really loud! Every time Shamer the Lie Monster whispers in your mind that you are bad, I need you to fight with all your heart and say, 'NO, I AM GOOD!' Can you tell Jingles and Stayshia that they believe lies too? Tell them they are precious and good."

I AM GOOD.

I AM GOOD.

I AM GOOD!

"I AM GOOD!"
Say it louder!

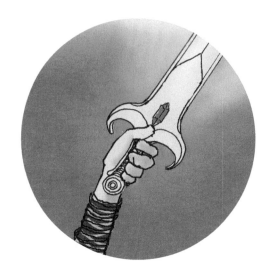

Shamer the Lie Monster has been struck a nasty blow. With his mask knocked off, any princess can see Shamer is weak and powerless once the truth is known. The distorted mirror he used to lie to Jingles and make her see bad things about herself is broken as well. Look closely at Jingles' sword. Shamer's jewel is now in her sword, and the power that he tried to steal from Jingles belongs to her once more.

CHAPTER 4

Lie #2
"It Was My Fault"

Now that Princess Gracie has begun helping Jingles understand that she is not bad, Jingles is beginning to feel a little better. However, the King is still concerned about Jingles because He knows she is being attacked by another one of the Deceiver's Lie Monsters named Guiltizar. He is just as ugly and mean as Shamer and his lies are just as cruel. He is an accuser[12] and loves to convince sweet children that it must be their fault when bad things happen, like if a mom and dad get divorced.

"I love you more than you could ever imagine!"
-The King

Jingles remembered what Mr. Finks said: "I knew you wanted me to touch you like this because of that big hug you gave me when you got here and the smile you gave me when you were eating the cookies. Then you flirted with me while we played with the pillows." Jingles was not sure what flirting meant, but she knew she was having fun. She laughed a lot and smiled at Mr. Finks. She even hit him lots of times with her pillow. After Guiltizar's vicious lies, precious Jingles thought, *I must have flirted so the touching and the yucky movie was all my fault.*

Princess Gracie is shouting, and very loudly I might add, "This is the hugest lie and it's as big as every chocolate chip cookie ever baked, which, if put side by side, would wrap around the earth a zillion times." I'm just saying this is a really big lie. Can you tell that the princess writing this book really loves chocolate chip cookies? I really do, but not as much as I love Jingles, and not as much as I love the precious princess reading this book. Just remember, according to the King's decree in John 3:16, He loves us a zillion times more than we could ever love each other or ever love chocolate chips cookies!![13] WOW, that's a lot of love!

How can we help Jingles know the truth that it was not her fault? What can Princess Gracie say to help Jingles know that when Mr. Finks showed her the

Have you ever felt WOOZEEKABOOZEE?

movie and touched her, it was not her fault? Let's help Jingles fight those nasty lies by finding the truth; this will help her heart and mind heal so she won't feel so woozeekaboozee. But why does she feel so guilty? Let's ask her and get to the bottom of this mystery.

Why does Jingles feel so guilty?

"Precious Jingles, I can see you're still missing some of your jingle. Can you tell me more about why you think it was your fault when Mr. Finks touched you, because it was NOT your fault," says Princess Gracie.

"But I know it's my fault because I just sat there the whole time while he touched me. I should have gotten up and run home. I should have kicked him and punched his lights out. I should never have hugged him or eaten his stupid cookies. They weren't even that great. He cheated and used the rolled up frozen kind," responds Jingles.

"Wow," said Princess Gracie. "You said a mouth full of 'I should haves.' I'm so proud of you for being brave and telling me how you feel. You have so many thoughts and feelings swirling around inside, and our Father the King sent me to help you sort out this mess. He sees your hurts and says He will heal your pain.[14] Tell me more about what you are thinking so we can fight it. Remember, the truth is what will help you heal. You will get your jingle back, which is how the Father made you, and you are one of the most jingly princesses the Father ever created."

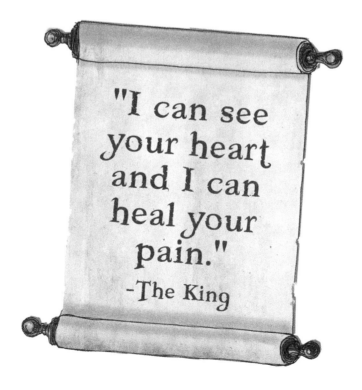

"I can see your heart and I can heal your pain."
-The King

"Ok," says Jingles, "I'll tell you what I hear in my head, but it sounds just like me and it seems true:

I should never have gone to Stayshia's house.

I should never have sat next to Mr. Finks on the sofa.

I should have moved his hand when he put it on my leg.

I should have left when I saw the girls take off their clothes on the TV."

Princess Gracie has special lie detecting powers from the Father and she said to Jingles, "Sweetheart, I'm sensing there is something else really big you're afraid to tell me. We can't fight Guiltizar unless we know all the lies you believe. What other thoughts make you especially sad? You are safe here and I love you no matter what you tell me."

"I will help you uncover lies so you can know the Truth."
-The King

Jingles refused to look at Princess Gracie and then blurted out, "I **really** should have screamed at Mr. Finks when I saw him put his.... I should have known he was hurting her... I should have..." and then Jingles allowed the sobs to come.

What are your "I should haves"?

Princess Gracie wrapped her arms around Jingles and said, "One day, you will understand that you really are a princess and none of this was your fault. You are royalty and a very valuable treasure to our Father and many others. You not only blame yourself for allowing Mr. Finks to touch you, but you also believe it is your fault that Stayshia got hurt. You are carrying some really ocean-sized lies in your tender heart, and only our Father is strong enough to help us fight Guiltizar the Lie Monster. Father will help us. Did you know in His decree, He says nothing can separate us from His love; not even death, far distances, evil monsters or anything?[15] It will take time, but the King sent me, your safe family, and your friends to help you feel better and get your jingle back.

What ocean-sized lies are you believing in your tender heart?

Let's help Jingles find the truth hidden behind all of the lies she believes. It is easy to see that Guiltizar is very good at being a Lie Monster. He is planting billions of lies, so he is going to be a tough monster to defeat. We're going to have to swing our Sword of

Truth back and forth a trillion times to defeat him. Jingles is being so brave by telling us what is hurting her heart, looking at her thoughts about what happened and choosing to control the way she thinks about it. The Father says by controlling our thoughts, we fight the enemies who want to destroy us.[16]

Princess Gracie says, "Let's look for clues to find the truth. Look back in the story when Mr. Finks said, 'I knew you wanted me to touch you like this because of that big hug you gave me when you got here and the smile you gave me when you were eating the cookies. Then you flirted with me while we played with the pillows.'"

CLUE Look at the picture on page 11. Did Jingles look like she wanted to be touched?

CLUE Do you think giving a person a hug means you want them to touch your private area?

CLUE Does eating cookies make everyone smile? DUH!! Every princess smiles when she gets to eat her favorite cookies.

CLUE Did you notice on page 6 that it says, "Mr. Finks always gives Jingles special gifts or treats"? Why would he do that?

CLUE Look at the pictures on page 9 and page 11. Does Jingles' face look as if she is glad Mr. Finks is touching her, or does she look really scared?

CLUE Is Jingles still excited about her birthday party? Why not?

Let's help Princess Gracie teach Jingles the real truth:

TRUTH "Jingles, you hugged Mr. Finks when you came in the door because you were happy and thankful to have a play date with Stayshia. You gave Mr.

Finks a hug because you are precious and loving. He has always been kind to you so there was no reason to be any different than your same sweet self. Hugs DO NOT mean you want someone to touch you in your private parts!"

TRUTH "Jingles, you smiled when you were eating chocolate chip cookies because you are one of the most wonderful and most beautiful princesses in the entire Kingdom. All princesses smile when eating their favorite snacks, and chocolate happens to be one of the best! A precious princess' smile does NOT mean you want someone to touch your private parts or show you a movie that makes you feel yucky inside."

TRUTH Mr. Finks gave Jingles "special gifts and treats" to trick her into thinking he cares about her. He also wanted her to keep the secret so the gifts were to cause Jingles to feel guilty if she told anyone.

TRUTH "Jingles, you did have a fun pillow fight with

Mr. Finks and Stayshia. You laughed and enjoyed every minute of it. Honey, the ability to laugh and play is one of our Father's greatest gifts to us. Your laughter is a joy to everyone that gets to hear it, and the Father loves to hear you laugh. Also, your playfulness is delightful and it makes healthy people feel happy and cared for. But in unhealthy people, when their mind is ill, they sometimes make bad choices.

The King says that Mr. Finks is in BIG trouble for hurting Jingles. The person who hurt you is in BIG trouble too, even if you don't ever see him or her punished.

Mr. Finks made very bad choices by touching you and Stayshia in your private areas. He also made a bad choice when he showed you the yucky movie. Princess Jingles, this is not your fault. You were feeling and behaving exactly like a precious princess. Mr. Finks is in big trouble for hurting you!"

Remember to get out the Sword of Truth to fight against these Lie Monsters.

Princess Gracie is getting out the Sword of Truth and says, "Jingles, it is time for you to hold this sword and begin practicing your battle to fight these lying enemies. I can help you. This will be a hard fight, but many other princesses are praying for you and cheering for you all over the world! The truth is that **it was not your fault—none of it was your fault.** You need to shout it out loud, hear it in your mind, and believe it in your heart. Let's hear you say it."

Jingles holds up the sword and shyly says, "It was not my fault."

"This is a good start," says Princess Gracie, "but Jingles, you need to say it like you mean it. Say it loud enough that the Lie Monster can't pretend not to hear you."

Jingles can feel a tiny bit of her jingle coming back. It really does help to know the truth.

Suddenly, as Jingles shouts, **"It was not my fault; I did not make Mr. Finks do those bad things to me,"** she can feel a tiny bit of her jingle coming back. She thinks, *It really does help to know the truth.*

Can you, Princess _____, also say, "It was not my fault!"?

CHAPTER 5

Lie #3
"I Am Dirty"

Wow, great work in fighting Guiltizar! He hates our Father the King very much and he knows the King loves His children more than anything else He created! Unfortunately, Guiltizar and Shamer will continue to try to destroy you during your whole, sweet royal life, but it will get easier over time and you will have help along the way. By the way, the King adores Stayshia just as much, and He is working on a special plan to rescue her as well.

Oh no! Princess Gracie is sensing another one of the Master Deceiver's troublesome liars named Ickylamar. She has a special gift about these things because someone not so nice touched her in bad ways too. She remembers feeling very guilty and very confused at the same time. Princess Gracie suspects Jingles could feel confused and guilty inside because sometimes it did not hurt when Mr. Finks touched her private area. Princess Gracie says, "I remember it sometimes felt good when grown-up people made wrong choices and touched me in my private places. That's what made me feel especially dirty. It also made me feel like I was bad, and it was my fault, and that I was the worst kid in the world. I never knew I was a princess back then!!"

Ickylamar will try to convince you that you are dirty and can never be clean.

Jingles is hearing Ickylamar the Lie Monster whisper, "I am dirty," over and over again in her mind. Jingles wants to soak for a long time in the bathtub

to get clean, but no matter how hard she scrubs, she doesn't feel like she can ever be clean again. Ickylamar the Lie Monster has taken over, and his lies are getting inside Jingles' heart and mind. Let's help fast.

Princess Gracie knows that Ickylamar is telling lies because she knows that **Jingles is truly squeaky clean already and very precious**. The Father made her that way! It's the truth; she's clean already. Just check out the King's decree in the section called Acts 15:9,[7] if you don't believe me.

What helps you feel clean?

Princess Gracie decides to have a princess-to-princess talk with Jingles about the Lie Monster Ickylamar. She explains, "Ickylamar is nasty and scummy and creepy and gross and slimy. Just look at his picture! He and his lies are nasty but you, Stayshia and all the other princesses who have been touched inappropriately are good and precious and clean! Just because your princess skin did not say "ouch" does not mean you are bad or dirty. It just means your skin is doing a good job detecting the world around it."

Princess Gracie knew that this was hard to understand, but she had learned so much from her wise Father the King, and she knew that she could explain it so that Jingles would understand. Princess Gracie said, "Jingles, you feel yucky in your tummy because sometimes it felt good when Mr. Finks touched your private parts." Princess Gracie wanted to teach Jingles and Stayshia some very important facts about our amazing bodies so that they will not feel those awful feelings anymore. Let's look at the truth. Why? Remember, the truth helps us stop believing the lies!!!

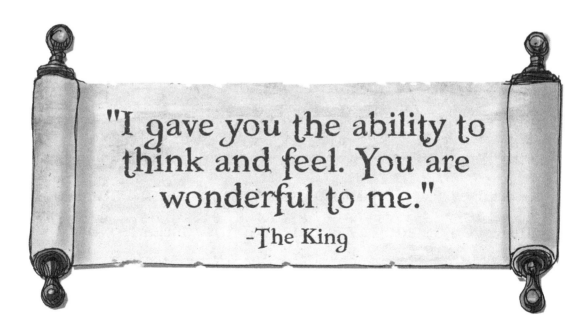

"I gave you the ability to think and feel. You are wonderful to me."
-The King

Remember when we discussed that you were carefully and wonderfully made? Well, our Father the King gave you, Jingles, and Stayshia the ability to feel things, such as hot, cold, or ticklish. He made our bodies to

The King gave you special skin detectors to help you stay safe and it is good!

feel lots of different things automatically without us being able to control it and this is good. For example, if you touched a hot stove, would you be able to control whether it hurt or felt good? No silly, that's a ridiculous question. If you held a piece of ice in your hand, could you decide to make it feel hot instead? No!

Decree Ps. 139:13 says the King gave your skin some special skin detectors that decide what to feel.[17] One purpose of these detectors is to keep you safe.

For example, if your hands get near a stove, your brilliant skin detectors tell your brain, "Hey, this is really hot, it hurts, pull away NOW!!" Some detectors are made for the purpose of good feelings. The King did not want you to only have the ability to feel pain, but also pleasure. Remember how good it feels when Stayshia runs up and gives you a hug or when you sit in your mom's lap and she holds you. The Father wanted hugs and touching to feel good when the hug is from someone safe who loves you.

Now Jingles understands how her body works and defeats Ickylamar's awful lies.

However, our skin does not know the difference when a safe and loving person is touching it or when someone like Mr. Finks is touching it. We princesses can't control the good feelings just like we can't control the pain when our skin gets hurt. You didn't do anything wrong and the good feelings are not your fault, just like it is not your fault that your knee hurts when you fall and scrape it. The King made it that way to protect you and it is good.

Can you say, "I am so squeaky clean, I shine?

Jingles now understood more about how her body works, and she felt grateful that Princess Gracie had the wisdom to teach her. Jingles was ready now to fight the awful lies that Ickylamar tried to make her believe. Without waiting for Princess Gracie to tell her, Jingles cried out, **"I am so squeaky clean, I shine. I am so clean that I am a reflection of my Father the King."** Princess Gracie was very proud of Jingles, and Jingles was proud of herself. The yucky

feeling was gone because it was the lies that made her feel dirty, and she no longer believed the lies.

CHAPTER 6

Lie #4 "I Must Have Liked It"

The last and most dangerous Lie Monster is Confusia. The King's decree in Ps. 5:9 warns us about the Master Deceiver's desire to destroy all princesses.[18] With Confusia's forked tongue, she whispers lies along with some facts and compliments into Jingles' heart. With all of this swirling around in a princess' mind, knowing what is the truth and what is a lie becomes very confusing, and it is easy to get tricked into believing the lies. Confusia looks so silly, sounds so kind, and it feels so good to listen to her voice. Sometimes what she says even starts out as the truth! After saying truthful and kind things, Confusia slowly twists the truth with evil lies, and then she twists in even more lies so that the only part coming out at the end is ALL LIES!! After listening to Confusia, Jingles will have thoughts in her mind and beliefs in her heart that make her hate herself and her

Confusia is the most dangerous Lie Monster! She mixes a little bit of truth with evil lies so that Jingles is completely confused.

King. It is the saddest thing ever!!! Confusia wants to steal all of the King's precious princesses away from Him permanently. All of Confusia's lies are cruel and cause hurt in a princess' heart. She will not be able to enjoy the special gifts her Father the King has for her

because she will not feel that she deserves anything good in her life. If Jingles believes Confusia the Lie Monster, she will begin believing she is worthless.

> ## Confusia tries to make Jingles feel worthless. How do lies make you feel about yourself?

Having lost her jingle, she won't feel like doing all the things she did before she got hurt like basketball, making brownies with mom, shopping at the mall, or doing homework with her friends. Believing lies can cause forever damage to a precious princess if she does not learn to fight each Lie Monster with the truth. Her grades may go down drastically so that she never goes to college or she may decide to quit the basketball team, which was a sport that brought her great joy.

Let's look at an example of how the Lie Monster Confusia takes a true statement and mixes it with a lie to make the whole message seem believable. Remember when Mr. Finks said, "I knew you wanted me to touch you like this because of that big hug you gave me." The truth part was Jingles did give Mr. Finks a hug because she trusted him and loved him. She had known Mr. Finks for a long time and he had always been kind. The lie part is that this meant Jingles wanted to be touched in her private area. It

> # How is your life different because of the abuse? Ask the King to heal your pain and restore those things taken.

was Mr. Finks who chose to tell this ugly lie when he wanted to do the wrong thing and touch Jingles. But Confusia the Lie Monster will keep reminding Jingles of the true part about how she happily gave Mr. Finks a hug so that Confusia can sneak in a vicious lie that Jingles liked being touched. This lie is so mean and if precious Jingles believes it, she will begin feeling guilt, shame, and other awful feelings.

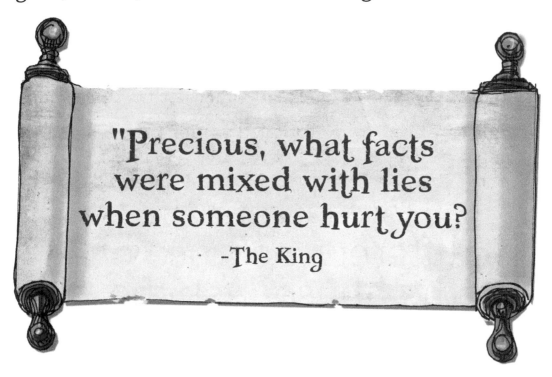

"Precious, what facts were mixed with lies when someone hurt you?
-The King

Now let's look at two examples of how Mr. Finks used compliments and being nice to gain Jingles' trust to see how Confusia can cause Jingles to believe lies, feel terrible pain in her heart, and stop trusting the King or His other children. One day, the King plans to cast Confusia into a lake of fire because she is so mean and hurts His kids.[19] Uh oh! Princess Gracie is getting mad and wants to bop Confusia on the head right now!

First, on page 10, Mr. Finks told Jingles she was very special and he wanted to be her special friend. The truth part is Jingles is special. This is such a confusing message. Mr. Finks was not telling Jingles she is special because he cared about her, but because he was doing something wrong and he wanted to continue. He was being kind to Jingles also and giving her compliments because he wanted her to keep a terrible secret. The secret Mr. Finks did not want Jingles to tell anyone was about the wrong things he was doing to her and to his stepdaughter Stayshia.

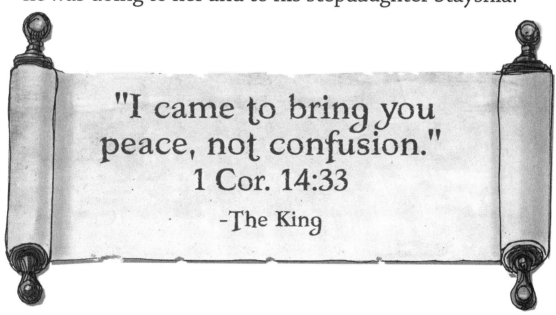

"I came to bring you peace, not confusion."
1 Cor. 14:33
-The King

Confusia the Lie Monster is whispering in Jingles' mind, "I'm his special friend and he said this is ok between special friends; it is our special secret." But sweet Jingles feels so yucky and dirty and scared and nervous in her tummy and heart. Sharing a secret with a friend can feel special, but what if someone is getting hurt? Can you see how Confusia mixes up everything?

"Never keep a secret from your mom, dad or safe friend if it is something that makes you feel yucky. I want you safe!
-The King

Second, on page 10, Mr. Finks said, "This is what good girls do and you are a very good girl." Mr. Finks used a compliment again to make Jingles cooperate and feel special. Saying these nice things to Jingles was a trick because Mr. Finks was hoping it would cause Jingles to trust him. Later, the Lie Monster Confusia will continue to try to trick Jingles by whispering things in her mind like, "I'm not a good girl," or "If that's what good girls have to do then I hate being a good girl." Jingles might start feeling angry at her own little sweet self when she remembers what Mr. Finks said and hears Confusia say, "I'm going to be a bad girl forever." If Confusia can make Jingles

Have you ever hurt yourself or someone else because of your anger and pain? If so, ask the people you hurt and the King for forgiveness and for Him to heal your pain."

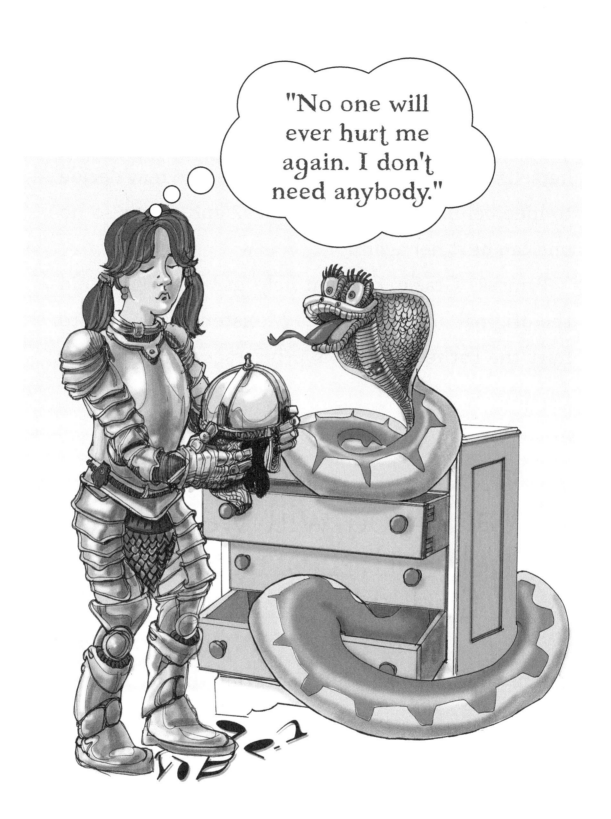

believe that she is bad already and can never be good again, then Jingles may end up doing bad things to herself and maybe to others too. She also may decide to hide behind an imaginary mask and armor so no one can hurt her again.

Princess Gracie, can you help us? Mr. Finks told the original lies, but the Lie Monsters always try to hurt the Father's precious princesses long after the

Maybe one day, when you get your own jingle back, you will want to help other princesses find the truth too.

bad touching happened by repeating the lies in their minds. Continuing to listen to and believe the Master Deceiver's lies will kill the music in Jingles' heart forever. She must take control of her thoughts and ask the King to show her the truth.[16]

Princess Gracie said, "My favorite thing to do is help other brave princesses figure out the truth, learn that they can heal, and find their jingle once more. Some of Confusia's lies are hard for any princess to figure out. Let's look for our clues. **Once you know the whole truth, you will be able to find your jingle inside.**"

When Mr. Finks told Jingles "You will like this," was he telling the truth or was he telling a lie?

CLUE How did Jingles feel when Mr. Finks touched her under her skirt?

CLUE On page 10, after the sentence "Jingles DID NOT FEEL SPECIAL," what did it say Jingles wanted to do?

CLUE Look at all the pictures of Jingles' face after she had been touched by Mr. Finks. Was Jingles smiling during the touching or did she look scared?

TRUTH The fact that Jingles felt so uncomfortable, so scared, so nervous and her tummy hurt is a clue that she did **NOT** like what was happening one bit!!

When Mr. Finks told Jingles she could not tell anyone about their special game because it would make Stayshia get in big trouble, he was telling a big fat lie! He was also telling a big fat lie when he said Stayshia would be taken to a bad and dangerous place called a foster home.

CLUE The biggest clue that Mr. Finks was telling a lie is when he said this is a "special secret" and no one could know about it, not even her mom or dad.

TRUTH All grown-ups know that it is wrong to tell a child to keep secrets from safe adults, especially from their parents.

TRUTH Mr. Finks used compliments to gain Jingles' trust and then told lies because he knew he would get into big, and I mean really big trouble, if Jingles told anyone about the very wrong things he was doing to both Stayshia and Jingles.

Was the person who touched you a stranger or someone you know? Would it make a difference?

I have an important question to ask you. Do you think it was harder for Jingles to sort out the truth because Mr. Finks was not a stranger, but someone she thought was her friend? How would it be different if a stranger touched her instead of Stayshia's stepfather?

Confusia the Lie Monster wants all of the King's

children to suffer so she speaks lies into their minds such as, "I can't tell anyone because it was my fault" or "I can't tell anyone because no one will believe me." Do you think Confusia might have lied to Jingles and

Were you ever afraid no one would believe you? Some people may not, but the King knows and can heal you.

said, "No one will believe you because Mr. Finks is so nice to everyone" or "No one believes kids, just adults"?

Most times when the people that we love or trust hurt us, the pain is more intense and is way more confusing because we don't expect to be hurt by someone who is supposed to care about and love us. It's hard to understand that someone who is kind and does nice things can also be cruel and do mean things. Confusia

the Lie Monster knows this and uses lies to create even more pain in our hearts. But guess what? We now know how to recognize the lies when they swirl around in our heads. We are smart and we are brave. Confusia has no power over Jingles anymore!

Through Princess Gracie's love and wisdom, Jingles has learned to trust what her body and feelings tell her. Sometimes our feelings are based on a lie we believe in our minds. By her willingness to examine her beliefs, talk to safe people about her feelings, and challenge her negative thoughts, Jingles gradually discovered the truth. By using these same tools throughout her life, she will be able to find her jingle every time she loses it.

So once again, Jingles picks up her Sword of Truth, and knowing now that she is special, that she is good, and that what Mr. Fink's did was wrong and not her fault, she exclaims in a very strong and jingly voice, ***"I am Princess Jingles, and I have found the truth!"***

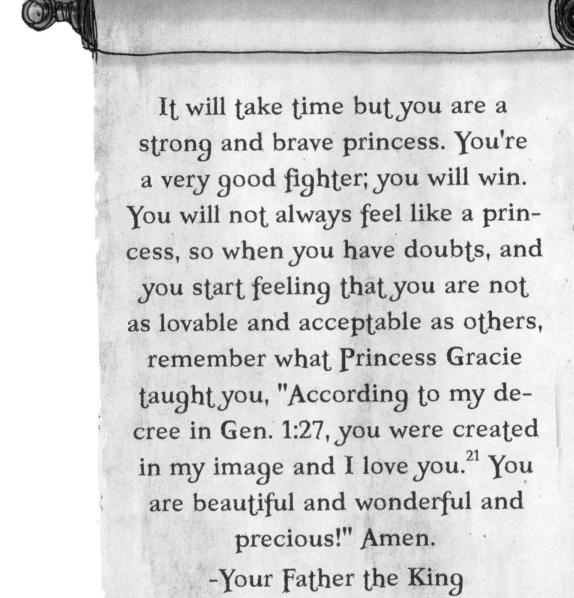

It will take time but you are a
strong and brave princess. You're
a very good fighter; you will win.
You will not always feel like a princess, so when you have doubts, and
you start feeling that you are not
as lovable and acceptable as others,
remember what Princess Gracie
taught you, "According to my decree in Gen. 1:27, you were created
in my image and I love you.[21] You
are beautiful and wonderful and
precious!" Amen.

-Your Father the King

CHAPTER 7

Now That You Know You Are A Princess

You've worked hard, and now you know how to fight the Lie Monsters... GOOD JOB! But sweetie, I am sad to say that the Lie Monsters will make sneak attacks at different times during your life. Their lies will sound like your own voice and will be the loudest whenever you make a mistake, and

Keep the Sword of Truth by your side at all times.

The Truth really does
set you free!

all us cute princesses make mistakes. You might need the help of a safe grown-up, and you can always pray for the King's help. You will also need to keep your Sword of Truth close by your side, so that you can fight them. You are a strong and brave princess, and a very good fighter; you will win.

P.S. If you want to know more about the King's deep love for you and your royalty, see Appendix VII.

Do's and Don'ts
Helpful instructions for adults

1) KEEP THE ROUTINE
Do get her back into her normal routine as soon as possible after the initial trauma. This will feel reassuring and comfortable because her routine is familiar and can offer a sense of safety and stability. It can reduce her stress, and help her feel she can manage her life again.

Don't baby her. <u>After the initial disclosure and a brief time to get over the shock,</u> it will be more helpful to her if she is not allowed to make new rules, disobey, or act-out without normal and reasonable consequences. You will feel a tug in your heart to coddle her, let her miss school, let her watch too much TV, let her have extra privileges or whatever else to make her "feel" better or help her escape the bad feelings. Perhaps these are tactics you would choose to comfort yourself or to avoid the difficult work ahead, especially if the work seems overwhelming.

2) RESPONSIBILITIES
Do expect your child to continue doing homework, household responsibilities, etc. You do not want her to begin using the abuse as an excuse to avoid life, problems, and responsibilities, which can easily become a pattern into adulthood. (I could write a book just on this issue.)

Don't make excuses for her!

3) AFFECTION

Do hold and hug your child often but be sensitive about her physical space. She may want lots of touch from Mom but shy away from Dad for a while, or she may want the reverse.

Don't force affection. Many parents will tell children something like "Go give Uncle Fred a hug." This can be very uncomfortable even for a child who has not been abused, but especially for a child who has been violated. Children need to be able to choose whom they feel safe enough to hug. Let it be natural and on her terms.

4) VERBAL SUPPORT

Do let her know you believe her. Your reassurance in this area is vital! Tell her the abuse was not her fault, she did not deserve what happened to her, and nothing has changed how you feel about her. This may seem like, "DUH, my child knows I still care," but your child has so many thoughts running through her mind, and many of them are not sensible or logical. She may believe something one moment and an hour later begin believing the lies again.

Don't make accusatory comments such as, "Why didn't you run?" or "Why didn't you just call me?" or "Why didn't you tell me sooner?" I can't emphasize this enough as they will cause further damage. These statements imply blame and will cause your child to feel shame and take on false guilt. She's already feeling guilty and thinking about those things now. Children are taught from birth to obey adults. Your princess may have been threatened to keep what happened to her a secret. Be understanding of the fact that she was in a situation that was beyond her capability of knowing how to handle. There are no good choices for a child in this situation. Also, she may have felt afraid, helpless, trapped, uncertain and overwhelmed with conflicting emotions. Things seem so different in hindsight.

5) CONFIDENTIALITY

Do be careful about sharing her story. This is huge! She needs to have as much power as possible over who knows what. Ask her questions like, "Can we tell Grammy about what happened to you?" I know there will be times when you need to share with family members and friends, but be sensitive about this. Even though other adults in my life knew it was not my fault, I was certain that it was. So when my story kept being told to more and more people, the shame and guilt grew. It was as if someone was telling people I had done the molesting or had been having voluntary sex with people. I believed without question that I was a whore and a prostitute by the time I was 8 years old.

Don't assume she wants everyone to know or that she wants to hide it from everyone. She has just lost a lot of her choices during the abuse. Choosing to whom to disclose and when gives her some of her power back. My mother told about my abuse to everyone who would listen in order to get attention for herself. It became her pain rather than mine. Try to keep your pain separate from hers.

6) SEX EDUCATION

Do make time to answer questions about sex, her body, emotions, etc. Your child may begin asking lots of strange questions. She may ask about bodily functions, feelings, and so much more. You don't know what strange stuff she has been told to get her to comply, so listen, pray, and try to answer honestly. Caution here, however, is warranted: *Don't give your child more information than she asks for.* The process of healing and of sex education is long-term, and children can only handle bits at a time—usually only what they ask about. Make sure you are comfortable with this topic as soon as possible.

Don't use silly names to describe something or to describe body parts. Be comfortable saying words like: vagina, penis, or breast.

7) ADDRESSING SHAME

Do try very hard not to sound shocked, annoyed or afraid of what she wants to talk about. Get comfortable with the topic of abuse and sex as soon as possible. A body naturally feels good when it is touched so children will carry a tremendous amount of guilt and shame. Do not use words such as sin when discussing body parts. God made our bodies to react to touch. Let your child know it was the abuser who did something wrong, not her precious body.

Don't let your imagination go crazy! After abuse, many parents start worrying about stuff like "will my child like boys or girls," or "now she will be promiscuous." Learn to trust your ability to help her heal, trust her ability to learn and accept the truth about what happened, and trust God to help you both. *Abuse does not have to be a life sentence of emotional instability, poor choices or broken families.*

8) DISCLOSURE

Do be comfortable if she remembers something and wants to share it with you. Stop whatever you are doing and be available at that moment. Don't wait until later because she may lose her nerve to disclose. Your willingness to stop what you are doing to listen also speaks volumes to her heart about the fact that you believe her, you care and her pain is valid. Remind her to share these things with her counselor also.

Do allow her to share at her own pace.

Do praise her for being brave as she discloses.

Do be patient and compassionate as she struggles with telling you what happened. She may not remember all that happened because of the stress she was feeling at the time of the abuse. She may be worried about upsetting you or she may be afraid of being blamed and getting into trouble. Another huge issue children have when trying to disclose about the abuse is that they lack the ability to understand what has happened, and therefore, may not be able to describe it. The child's therapist is trained to help her sort through the memories, feelings and beliefs in order to heal. Your ability to listen and provide unconditional love is just as important!

Don't ask leading questions. See Appendix II for examples of leading questions.

How to Talk to Your Child If You Suspect Abuse

Remain calm, patient, and nonjudgmental to help your child feel safe and secure. Your tone, facial expression, and the way you behave will affect your child more than your words. Your goal is to reduce the fear and anxiety that your child may be experiencing while he or she is talking about the abuse.

Your goal is to reduce fear and anxiety, provide comfort and safety.

It is important that you are accepting of your child's feelings, *whatever they may be*.

Remember that it is the person who touched your child inappropriately that is to blame for the abuse. Your child is not to blame, *regardless of the circumstances*.

During your conversation with your child, comfort your child with the healing words **"I believe you,"** "It is not your fault," "I love you no matter what," and "I will take care of you."

Know that inappropriate touching can sometimes feel good to your child. Asking them if they were hurt may not address what has happened to them.

If your child tells you that they made a promise not to tell, help your child understand when it is not ok to keep a secret. For example, if someone made them feel bad or uncomfortable then it is **always** ok to tell.

Disclosure is difficult. You can help your child by making supportive statements such as "What else happened?" "I won't be mad at you," "I want to protect you," "You are brave," and "Take your time."

If you suspect abuse, ask open-ended questions. In other words, do not suggest what might have happened in the questions you ask. Allow your child to supply the information. Here are some examples:

Do ask: "Who made you feel bad or made you do something you didn't like?"

Don't ask: "Did your swim coach touch you?"

Do ask: "What happened?"

Don't ask: "Were you touched in your private parts?"

Do ask: "When did this happen?" (Note: 'When' type questions are difficult for children under 5 years old)

Don't ask: "Did this happen yesterday evening?"

Do ask: "Where did this happen?"

Don't ask: "Did this happen at your friend's house?"

Don't ask the same questions over and over again. Children are suggestible, and may feel that they gave the wrong answer. Your child will want to please you by telling you what they think you want to hear.

This revelation will be upsetting and disturbing to you. Regardless of the feelings you are facing, your focus must be on remaining calm and helping her feel heard, safe, and comforted. Refrain from impulsively reacting or confronting the abuser. Do not allow further contact of any kind between the abuser and child and contact the authorities.

Your goal is to gather basic information, not conduct an investigation. After asking the questions listed above, if you suspect abuse, do not let your child have contact with the abuser, and contact your local authorities.

Keep a record of the dates of your child's disclosures, and what was disclosed. Use your child's own words as much as possible. Also, keep records of all communication you have with respect to the suspected abuse. This includes dates and times, names and telephone numbers, and notes of each conversation with helpers and authorities.

Safety Rules for Children

Knowing My Rules for Safety

I CHECK FIRST

with my parents, guardians, or other trusted adults before going anywhere, doing anything, helping anyone, accepting anything, getting into a vehicle, or leaving with anyone.

I TAKE A FRIEND

with me when going places or playing outside.

I TELL SOMEONE NO

if they try to touch me or do things in ways that make me feel scared, uncomfortable, or confused, because it's OK for me to stand up for myself.

I TELL MY PARENTS, GUARDIANS, OR OTHER TRUSTED ADULTS

if anything happens to me.

How Do I Teach My Child About Personal Safety?

A Letter From *Nancy McBride*

National Safety Director for The National Center for Missing and Exploited Children

Many parents and guardians feel challenged to keep their children safer in our fast-paced and global society. They may wonder at what age they can begin teaching their children about personal safety.

Unfortunately, "one size" doesn't fit all. A child's ability to understand safety skills and put them into practice is determined not just by age, but also by the child's educational and developmental levels. To truly learn new safety skills, children need to model, rehearse and practice the skills to incorporate them into their daily lives.

- Speak to your child in a calm and reassuring way. Fear is not an effective teaching tool; confidence is.

- Speak openly about safety issues. If you approach child safety openly, your children will be more likely to come to you with problems or concerns.

- Don't confuse children by warning against "strangers." Danger to children is much greater from someone you or they know than from a "stranger."

- Teach children that no one has the right to force, trick, or pressure them into doing things they don't want to do.

- Practice safety skills by creating "what if" scenarios. An outing to a mall or the park can serve as a chance for children to practice safety skills, such as checking with you before they go anywhere or do anything, and locating adults who can help if they need assistance.

- Supervise your children. It is vital to their protection and safety. Children should not be put in the position of making safety choices if they are not old enough or skilled enough to make those choices.

- Check out adults who have access to your children. The more involved you are in your child's life, the less likely it is that your child will seek attention from other, potentially dangerous adults.

SIMPLE RULES FOR CHILDREN WHEN THEY NEED HELP

The National Center for Missing & Exploited Children (NCMEC) has a signature safety publication, *Knowing My Rules for Safety,* to help parents and guardians teach personal safety skills to children. The rules are simple and concise and provide encouragement and options for children who need an adult's help

Finding A Therapist and Other Resources

There are several ways to find a therapist. Here are some options.

THERAPISTS

- National Board for Certified Counselors
www.nbcc.org/counselorfind

Go to this site and click on your state. You will be presented with a list of certified counselors in the state you selected. On the left hand side of the page, filter on *Areas of Practice* and select *Sexual Abuse Recovery*. Now select *Search Filter*, optionally enter a zip code, and click *Apply*.

- Local psychological or psychiatric association referral services
- University departments of psychology or psychiatry
- Child exploitation hotlines
- Child protective services agencies
- Rape crisis or sexual assault centers
- Family court services of court appointed special advocate (CASA) groups
- Crime victim assistance programs in the law enforcement agency or prosecutor's (district attorney's) office.

RESOURCES

National Center for Missing & Exploited Children (NCMEC)

A non-profit organization with a mission to serve as the nation's resource on the issues of missing and sexually exploited children, providing information and resources to law enforcement, parents, and children including child victims as well as other professionals.

> Charles B. Wang International Children's Building
> 699 Prince Street
> Alexandria, Virginia 22314-3175
> The United States of America
> **www.missingkids.com**

> **24-HOUR HOTLINES**
> Phone: 703-224-2150
> Fax: 703-224-2122
> 1-800-THE-LOST (1-800-843-5678)

VOICE Today

A non-profit organization breaking the silence & cycle of child sexual abuse through awareness, prevention and healing programs and resources. For more information please visit **www.voicetoday.org**

Bible References

All verses are copied from *Bible Gateway* in Easy-To-Read version

1. John 8:44 - Your father is the devil. You belong to him. You want to do what he wants. He was a murderer from the beginning. He was always against the truth. There is no truth in him. He is like the lies he tells. Yes, the devil is a liar. He is the father of lies.

2. John 10:10 - A thief comes to steal, kill, and destroy. But I came to give life—life that is full and good.

3. John 8:32 - You will know the truth, and the truth will make you free."

4. Psalms 18:16-19 - He reached down from above and grabbed me. He pulled me from the deep water. He saved me from my powerful enemies, who hated me. They were too strong for me, so he saved me.
    They attacked me in my time of trouble, but the Lord was there to support me. He was pleased with me, so he rescued me. He took me to a safe place.

5. Matthew 19:14 - But Jesus said, "Let the little children come to me. Don't stop them, because God's kingdom belongs to people who are like these children."

6. Romans 8:1 - So now anyone who is in Christ Jesus is not judged guilty.

7. Acts 15:9 - To God, those people are not different from us. When they believed, God made their hearts pure.

8. 2 Corinthians 10:4-6 - The weapons we use are not human ones. Our weapons have power from God and can destroy the enemy's strong places. We destroy people's arguments, and we tear down every proud idea that raises itself against the knowledge of God. We also capture every thought and make it give up and obey Christ. We are ready to punish anyone there who does not obey, but first we want you to be fully obedient.

9. Psalms 139:14 - I praise you because you made me in such a wonderful way. I know how amazing that was!

10. Matthew 19:14 - If one of these little children believes in me, and someone causes that child to sin, it will be very bad for that person. It would be better for them to have a millstone tied around their neck and be drowned in the deep sea.

11. Jeremiah 29:11 - I say this because I know the plans that I have for you." This message is from the Lord. "I have good plans for you. I don't plan to hurt you. I plan to give you hope and a good future."

12. Revelation 12:10 - Then I heard a loud voice in heaven say, "The victory and the power and the kingdom of our God and the

authority of his Messiah have now come. These things have come, because the accuser of our brothers and sisters has been thrown out. He is the one who accused them day and night before our God."

13. John 3:16 - Yes, God loved the world so much that he gave his only Son, so that everyone who believes in him would not be lost but have eternal life.

14. Job 36:15 - God saves those who suffer by using their suffering. He uses their troubles to speak in a way that makes them listen.

15. Romans 8:38 - Yes, I am sure that nothing can separate us from God's love—not death, life, angels, or ruling spirits. I am sure that nothing now, nothing in the future, no powers, nothing above us or nothing below us—nothing in the whole created world—will ever be able to separate us from the love God has shown us in Christ Jesus our Lord.

16. 2 Corinthians 10:5 - And we tear down every proud idea that raises itself against the knowledge of God. We also capture every thought and make it give up and obey Christ...

17. Psalms 139:13 - You formed the way I think and feel. You put me together in my mother's womb.

18. Psalms 5:9 - My enemies never tell the truth. They only want to destroy people. Their words come from mouths that are like open graves. They use their lying tongues to deceive others.

19. 1 Corinthians 14:33 - God is not a God of confusion but a God of peace...

20. Revelation 19:20 - But the beast was captured, and the false prophet was also captured. He was the one who did the miracles for the beast. He had used these miracles to trick those who had the mark of the beast and worshiped its idol. The false prophet and the beast were thrown alive into the lake of fire that burns with sulfur.

21. Genesis 1:27 - So God created humans in his own image. He created them to be like himself. He created them male and female.

I Prayed and I Love God Why Did I Still Get Hurt

God's plan was not for any of us to be abused, sick or in pain. Satan began telling his lies a very long time ago so now everyone on earth experiences pain, sickness and so much more. One of the main ways we can fight Satan is by not listening to his lies and agree with what God says in the Bible.

I loved Jesus all my life and I prayed almost everyday. I could not figure out why Jesus let me get hurt and why the pain would not leave for many years after the abuse. The problem was, I really believed the enemy's lies after people hurt me. The lies I believed did more damage to my heart, soul and mind than the actual abuse. My body healed fast but the damage inside lasted for many years until I learned the truth.

Have any Bible verses ever seemed confusing? Many of the verses in the Bible confused me! But eventually, the Bible helped me heal once I understood what the verses meant. Let's look at some examples that will help you heal once you know the truth.

Genesis 1:27 - So God created humans in his own image. He

created them to be like Himself. He created them male and female.

This means God created you and He wanted you to be like Him. Have you ever noticed moms and dads love to say, "she has my eyes" or "he has my nose." They are proud to have their child look like them. God created you to be like Him and planned your life to be amazing and easy and without pain. So what happened?

Satan began lying to God's children! Psalms 5:9 says, My enemies never tell the truth. They only want to destroy people. Their words come from mouths that are like open graves. They use their lying tongues to deceive others.

Satan or the devil is the ultimate liar. He told big lies to Adam and Eve and they believed him instead of God. Believing his lies made their lives very hard which stole their jingle. Their kids and the kids of their kids all the way to us have believed the same lies. If moms, dads, neighbors, friends, teachers and most everyone else have no joy because they believe the mean things Satan says, they will make very bad decisions. Some make decisions to fight, yell, lie, steal, and much more. Their life will be very hard until they believe the original truth—that God loves them very much even when they make big mistakes.

After the abuse, the pain in my physical body went away, but the pain in my heart and mind lasted a very long time! I believed I was damaged forever, the abuse was my fault and I would always be dirty. I also believed God did not care about me and could never love me. That's the biggest lie in the whole world and universe. Satan was very tricky in convincing me to believe his lies for so long. However, after getting counseling, learning more about God's love for me, learning how to fight Satan when he tells me lies, and praying, God healed my heart and mind.

I am now one of the most happy, most jingly princesses you would ever meet! I love you dear one and I am praying your jingle comes back very soon. You are precious, so fight hard!

CPSIA information can be obtained at www.ICGtesting.com
Printed in the USA
LVOW02s0409041213

363831LV00002B/3/P